ADALEE

CURVY GIRLS CAN

SADIE KING

LET'S BE BESTIES!

A few times a month I send out an email with new releases, special deals and sneak peeks of what I'm working on. If you want to get on the list I'd love to meet you!

When you join you'll get access to all my bonus content which includes Allie, a short and steamy romance in the Curvy Girls Can series.

Sign up here:
authorsadieking.com/bonus-scenes

ADALEE

CURVY GIRLS CAN BOOK THREE

A plus size model in a steamy short instalove romance.

Adalee

They call me the Viking Ice Queen—a fierce, plus-size model who refuses all men. Until I meet Hayden.

He watches me through the lens and it makes me feel beautiful, confident, and bold, bold enough to do something I know I shouldn't…

But when the one man I let in shatters my trust, will I ever let him close again?

Hayden

Since the moment I saw Adalee on the fashion runway, I've known she'll be mine. And now that I've got her in my photography studio, I'm not letting her go.

But it's not just her curves I crave. I want her heart, body, and soul.

Will she open herself to love, or has the Viking Ice Queen frozen me out of her heart?

Adalee is part of the Curvy Girls Can series—short,

steamy, and swoon-worthy instalove stories featuring confident women and the men who worship them.

Always high heat, always sweet, and always happily ever after. Each book is a standalone and can be read in any order.

ADALEE

My thighs burn as I perch on the side of the boat. Well, half a boat. I've been semi squatting in six-inch heels for the last hour, and my body's starting to feel it.

A single bead of sweat trickles down my neck and rolls all the way down into my cleavage, tickling my skin as it progresses. It does nothing to help the already hard nipple situation.

I squint into the lights. "I could do with a quick break."

Hayden lowers the camera, his deep blue eyes peering out from behind the lens.

"Let's take five."

His assistant rushes forward with a robe, but I wave it away. My body's on fire, and it's got nothing to do with the lights that are pointed on me.

I step out from the set and make my way to the

restroom. I lock the door behind me and lean my head against the cool wall.

"Get it together, girl," I mutter to myself. "Don't blow this job."

I long to splash cool water on my face, but the make-up artist spent two hours getting me ready, and she'll kill me if I come back with my face smudged.

Instead I go back out to the studio and the crew waiting for me.

Hayden hands me a bottle of water. "You look hot under there. You okay?"

"Sure," I lie. "I hope my make-up isn't running."

"You look perfect."

He smiles, and my god it sends a shiver all the way between my legs via my pebbled nipples. Those dimples, that shaggy hair, the way his artist's eyes roam over me, critical and appreciative like I'm a lost Rembrandt.

This is why I'm hot, this is why my nipples are hard under the swimsuit, and this is why everyone warns you about photographers.

"You really know how to work the camera," he says, and my stomach does a little flippity-flop. I know it's a line and one I've heard a million times in my six-year modeling career, but I don't mind hearing it from him.

"Thanks."

"I mean it. I'm not trying to be sleazy. You have something about you..."

We're interrupted by the stylist coughing and

looking pointedly at her watch. "Are we ready to move onto the cream two-piece?"

Hayden strides lazily over to his laptop, which is set up on a small table next to the camera.

"Are you happy with the shots of the blue swimsuit?" he asks Barry, the client. Barry's squinting at the laptop, flicking through the images we've just taken. "I think you've got something special here," adds Hayden, glancing back at me.

Barry nods. "Let's move on."

I follow the stylist into the dressing room, trying to calm my inflamed body.

This is what my mother warned me about when I started modeling. "Watch out for the sleazy photographers," she said.

She was a model in the 90s and knew what she was talking about.

I've watched the girls I work with fall into bed with the photographers, the agents, the male models who aren't gay, and even some of the gay ones too. It's an industry where sex sells, and it's used as currency to get to the top.

I'm determined not to fall into that trap. I was warned I'd lose jobs if I didn't sleep with the men who ran the industry, but I was willing to take that chance. There were some that was true of, who, after I rejected their advances, stopped booking me for jobs. But most just shrugged their shoulders and still booked me for work.

So while my model friends were sleeping their way through every man in the industry, I shut up shop. I went the other way, which is why I'm twenty-three years old and still a virgin.

I've never fallen for a photographer's charms. Until today.

The regular photographer, Sophie, is ill today and Hayden's the replacement. I'm used to Sophie. We're from the same small town, Maple Springs, and have known each other for years. We helped each other out when we first moved to Seattle, sharing advice on how to make it in this cutthroat world. She introduced me to the Maple Springs Businesswomen's network and those smart women have helped me run my modeling career like a business.

I wish Sophie were here today. She always makes me look fabulous and I'm relaxed around Sophie, unlike Hayden who's got my body overheating. Sophie doesn't have deep blue eyes, a tight t-shirt hugging hard muscles, and a mischievous smile that seems just for me.

Twenty minutes later, I'm back under the lights in a cream bikini, with my make-up refreshed, and the perspiration blotted off my neck.

Someone removed the half-boat and replaced it with a bar stool. I perch on the side and am handed a fake cocktail, complete with an umbrella and a candied cherry.

"Sit up straight, I don't want to see your stomach rolls," says Barry, still staring at the laptop.

I look down and take a moment to let the comment wash over me. I've been in this game long enough to develop a thick skin.

People regard models as objects to show off their clothes and forget we're people with feelings, especially plus size models. And when they're watching you from a laptop screen, they forget you're in the room.

"You need to apologize to Adalee."

My neck snaps up. Hayden is leaning over Barry's table staring at him. A red vein pulses in his neck; all signs of the charming photographer are gone.

Barry looks shocked. He stares at Hayden for a moment, and I hold my breath, wondering if they're going to get into an argument. But Hayden is wearing a don't fuck with me expression and Barry wisely backs down.

"I'm sorry, man. You're right, that wasn't a thoughtful comment."

Hayden straightens up, and Barry leans out from his chair so he can see me. "Sorry, Adalee." He smiles weakly. "I didn't mean any offense."

"It's okay." I give him a forgiving smile. He is the client after all. "I'll try not to slouch." I take a deep breath and silently forgive Barry for being an asshole.

"You want me to sit on the stool or lean on it?"

"Try leaning."

I strike a pose.

Barry sighs in frustration, as if I should be able to read his mind. "No, other side."

I move my position.

"Yeah, that's better."

"Can I suggest something?" Hayden doesn't wait for an answer but starts walking toward me. "Move your elbow like this."

He takes my arm and gently nudges it forward. His touch is electric, and heat emanates from where he's touching me. Just having him close makes me hot again, which will make me sweaty and ruin my makeup.

"Are you okay?" he whispers.

I glance up into his deep blue eyes, full of concern. "Yeah," I whisper. "I'm tougher than I look."

He smiles and there's warmth in his eyes. "You look pretty tough to me." He goes back to his place behind the camera.

The memory of his touch runs through my body, and I'm worried I'm leaving damp panty marks in this swimsuit. My heart is still racing when I hear the click of the camera.

"Look directly at me," says Hayden.

I turn to the lens, thinking about what I'd like to do to the man behind it.

"That's it. Perfect."

With Hayden on my mind and his touch imprinted on my body, I give him some poses as he snaps away.

My body moves to the rhythm of his camera. I feel beautiful, I feel sexy, and I'm in deep trouble.

My body moves to the rhythm of his camera. I feel beautiful, I feel sexy, and I'm in deep trouble.

2

HAYDEN

I watch Adalee pose in the cream two-piece, her hair slicked back and her body glistening. She looks down the lens with her intense gaze and pouty lips that make my dick ache. My fingers are slick with sweat, making it hard to press the shutter button.

I've been waiting a long time to work with Adalee Lane. Ever since I saw her on the fashion runway a year ago, I've been captivated by her.

She was modeling the plus size range for a top fashion house. When she came down the runway, I couldn't breathe. She's stunning, tall and voluptuous with golden hair that falls down her back. She's got a confidence and grace about her, and her larger size gives her a presence that can't be ignored.

The Viking Ice Queen, they call her. "Because she won't sleep with anyone," one of the other photographers told me. "Because she won't sleep with you, you mean," I'd said.

I like that about her. Adalee isn't like the other models. She's got an innocence about her that makes her sexier on camera and in the flesh.

"Lean forward for me," Barry tells her.

She does, and I'm given a full view of her cleavage. Two beautiful soft mounds with a deep hollow I'd love to explore.

Barry whistles softly, and my neck throbs with anger.

"Straighten up," I say tightly.

Barry gives me a dirty look. "Your brand doesn't show that much cleavage," I mutter.

I take a few more pictures, but I already know I've got the shot.

"I think we're done." I turn to Barry. "If you're happy, that is."

He flicks through the latest images on the laptop, studying each shot. He looks up and nods. "We're done for the day. Thanks everyone."

Adalee strides off set, an assistant trailing after her.

"Wouldn't mind a piece of that action," Barry says watching her go.

My fists clench as an inexplicable possessiveness flares inside me. "Don't talk about her like that."

Barry's eyebrows shoot up in surprise. "You like her or something?"

That's a fucking understatement. I've been obsessed

with Adalee for the past year. But I'm not going to share my feelings with this asshole. "You should show more respect to the models."

Barry takes in my size and the throbbing veins in my neck and wisely holds his hands up in surrender. "Dude. Calm down. I didn't mean any offense."

I stare at him for a few moments as my breathing gets under control. It's not a good look to punch a client in the face but if he tries to lay a finger on Adalee, that's what I'll do.

Barry chuckles. "You're wasting your time." He slaps me on the shoulder as he walks past. "You won't get the Viking Ice Queen into bed."

My fists clench again, but I let it go. I don't know what it is about this woman that brings out my possessive instincts. I've never felt so protective over a woman or lusted after one so much.

As a fashion photographer I've had plenty of opportunities with women, but easy sex has never appealed to me. I want a connection with the person I'm with.

People think I have an amazing job, photographing swimsuit models all day. But usually I can be objective, see them as props in the set that I need to work with.

Until today. Looking down the lens at Adalee in her swimsuit, I've had an uncomfortable boner since she walked onto set at 7 a.m. this morning.

I'm packing up my lenses when she comes out of the dressing room. She looks just as gorgeous in jeans and a sweater as she did in designer swim wear.

She's lugging a heavy bag behind her.

"I'll walk you to your car." I take the bag of her and she smiles her thanks.

"You were great today," I follow her out of the studio trying to wrench my gaze from her swaying hips and perfect ass. "They've got some good shots to work with."

She crinkles up her nose. "Thanks, but you know..." She trails off and shrugs her shoulders.

"No I don't know." I hope she's not worried about how she looks because she's fucking gorgeous and my camera loved her.

"It was only fashion work. I'm hardly changing people's lives."

I stop walking, and she turns to look at me. "You want to do more meaningful work?"

"Yeah. Something where I'm more than an object to show off a swimsuit."

"I know exactly what you mean."

My mind's racing as we start walking again. I've dreamed of photographing Adalee Lane for so long, really photographing her, and now I might just have a chance. "I'm working on some portraiture photography in my private studio. It's more artistic, more thoughtful than fashion photography."

"Is that what you'd really like to do?" she tilts her head to regard me curiously.

"Yeah. I would. I'd like to do something more meaningful too."

She nods. Her golden hair bounces over her shoulders, and I resist the urge to run my fingers through it. "I was wondering if you'd pose for me?"

She stops walking again. "I don't do nudes."

I chuckle. People always assume the worst in this business. "Artistic doesn't always mean nudes."

She raises an eyebrow like she doesn't believe me. "Really?"

"It means capturing people as they are, reflecting real life back through the lens of a camera."

She looks thoughtful, and I press on. "You've got a great presence. Would you pose for me?"

She hesitates, and I hold my breath. If she says no I'll be crushed. I've waited my entire life for someone like Adalee. I want to photograph her to get to know her, to penetrate her icy exterior and get to the passionate woman beneath.

"No nudes?"

"No nudes," I promise.

She nods. "Sure. I'll do it."

I can't help the grin that spreads across my face. "Perfect. Are you free tomorrow?"

"I've got an audition in the morning, but I could do the afternoon."

"Come to my studio at one."

I put her bag in the trunk of her car, and as I watch her drive off, I experience a joy I haven't felt in a long time. Tomorrow I will have Adalee Lane in my studio with no sleazy clients and no fussy make-up artists. Just the two of us and my lens.

3
ADALEE

’m still wondering what the hell I’ve agreed to as I press the buzzer to Hayden’s studio the next afternoon. He greets me with a grin which shows off his dimples and sets my heart racing.

It’s just the two of us today, and being alone with him makes me suddenly self-conscious.

“How was the audition?” he asks as he makes a pot of coffee.

I screw my nose up thinking about the brightly lit room and my audition piece. “Not great.”

His eyes shoot up expectantly. “How so?”

“The audition itself went fine; I was happy with it. But I’m tired of going for the same old roles.”

He pulls two mugs from the top shelf of the studio kitchen and as his t-shirt lifts up I glimpse ink under his shirt. “Are these acting parts?”

Hayden seems generally interested and I find

myself opening up to him. "I've been trying to break into acting. I'm tired of the modeling scene. But there aren't many parts for a girl like me."

He hands me a cup of coffee. "You mean for a beautiful, sophisticated, confident woman?"

I love it that my size isn't the first thing Hayden sees. I've been described as "plus size" for my entire career, defined and categorized by the shape of my body. I'm proud of my body and my curves, but there's a lot more to me than just my shape.

"I mean a curvy girl." I clarify.

"What was the audition for today?"

"Girl eating ice cream in cafe." I sigh. "Just once I'd like to audition for a part where I actually have a name. And where I wasn't eating."

"It's a waste of your talents. You've got an incredible look on camera."

You get used to compliments as well as criticism in this industry but coming from Hayden it makes my heart beat a little faster and a hot flush run up my neck.

I turn away quickly before he sees.

"What did you have in mind today?" I ask, changing the subject.

He takes a while to answer, and when I glance up, he's studying me with his intense gaze that makes me tingle all over.

"I want to capture you in a portrait. Something different than the fashion shots. Something more real."

He takes a step toward me. "There's something

about you, Adalee. A quality. I've never met anyone before who I've wanted to photograph so much."

My heart's beating a tattoo against my chest, but this is exactly what I've been warned about. He's probably had a hundred girls in here, and he's probably said this line a hundred times.

I give a short laugh. "Do you say that to all the models?"

His face turns serious. "No. Never."

I want to believe him, but my mother's warning runs through my head. I should turn and leave; I shouldn't have come here at all.

But he's looking at me so intensely, with his hair flopping around his eyes that I'm dying to run my fingers through. So instead I find myself nodding and asking him what he wants me to wear.

We choose an over-sized off the shoulder sweater and a pair of leggings. When I'm in the changing room, I decide at the last minute not to wear a bra. My breasts hang heavy underneath the sweater, but it looks better sliding off my bare shoulder.

I do light, natural make-up which feels good compared to the thick layers the make-up artists usually smear on.

I come out of the changing room, and Hayden nods appreciatively. "Perfect."

There's a simple loveseat in the studio with a gray shag-pile rug on the studio floor.

"I want you to sit on the couch. I thought we could talk while I take the photos so you're nice and relaxed."

I take a seat. "Do you mind if I take my shoes off?"

"I want you to do whatever feels natural."

I kick them off and roll my feet into the soft rug. It feels divine, and I close my eyes. I hear the click of the lens and open them again.

"You look good. Natural."

I smile. "Actually, I'd like to sit on the rug if that's okay."

"That's great."

I slide off the couch so my back's leaning against it as I sit on the rug. He adjusts some lights and takes a few shots.

It's warm under the lights, but I feel good, relaxed with just me and him.

"What would be the ideal acting part for you?" he asks.

I think for a moment, hearing the click of the camera lens. "Right now, I'd just like a speaking part that isn't related to my size."

"And eventually? What's the big dream?"

"Eventually, I'd like to break into interesting TV roles. Something with a bit of meat to it, a police-woman or a lawyer in a gritty drama or a single mom. But those kinds of roles don't seem open to girls like me."

"They should be. I'd be glued to the screen."

I smile, and he clicks the lens. "How about you?" I ask. "What's your big dream?"

"I'd like to open my own gallery. Do portraiture photography. I do a bit now, but I have to do fashion to pay the bills."

He crouches down so his lens is on a level with me. "Do you mind if I get down here?"

I shake my head. He lies down on the rug, and he's so close. I'm sure he can hear my heart hammering in my chest. Knowing he's watching me so intensely has my body tingling all over. I'm getting hot between the legs, and it's getting damp down there.

His lens follows me as I lean forward. My sweater hangs off my bare shoulder, and I feel sexy as hell as he clicks the lens.

I lean to the side so it slips down a bit more, showing not only my shoulder but the top of my breast.

There's an intake of breath, and he clicks the lens. I feel seductive and sexy knowing I'm having an effect on him.

"That's good," he breathes. "You look powerful."

I lean a bit more, letting the top slide a bit further. But it slips down more than I intended, and suddenly my whole breast is on display, nipple and all.

He gasps. And I should sit up, but instead I stare directly down his lens.

He doesn't click the camera. Instead he peers at me from behind the lens. "Your breast is showing."

Feeling brazen and powerful and daring, I look him dead in the eye. "I know."

He swallows, and a bead of sweat trickles down his forehead.

"Are you okay with me taking a picture like this, just for me?"

My heart beats against my breast and I should say no, but I feel daring with Hayden. I feel bold and this feels right. "I trust you."

He adjusts the lens, and I shift my gaze so I'm looking straight down it, powerful and strong and unafraid. He clicks a few times, and I change my position. My nipple hangs just over the top, grazing the fabric, and I feel it harden as I look down the lens.

I've never done anything like this before, so brazen and wanton. It goes against everything I've done in my career. But it seems so right with him.

I'm damp between the legs, and my breathing is shallow as he takes another photo.

Slowly, he puts the camera aside.

"Adalee, you're beautiful."

I can only stare at him as he crawls across the floor, until he's kneeling in front of me.

Our eyes are locked together, and I see my own desire reflected back in his.

He reaches out a hand and cups my breast. His thumb grazes my nipple. A delightful shiver travels through my body, and I close my eyes and lean back.

His lips press against my throat and move upward to find my lips.

He kisses me hard, and I kiss him back. My mother's warning flashes into my head, and I banish it to the back of my mind as my body takes over.

4

HAYDEN

I kneel before her, this Rubenesque goddess.

My mouth presses into hers, pulling her lips into mine. My hand cups her heavy breast, brushing her nipple with my thumb.

I've been watching Adalee for the last half an hour through the lens, my blood getting hot and my dick growing hard. She's the most beautiful woman I've ever seen.

When I asked to photograph her, that's all I wanted to do. But as soon as her sweater slipped off her shoulder, exposing that one perfect breast, I knew I would make her mine today.

I pull at her sweater and lift it over her head. I'm hungry for her, and my mouth moves over her soft skin to find a nipple. She gasps as I swirl the hard nub around my tongue, savoring the salty sweet taste.

My dick presses against my jeans, impatient to

make her mine. Her body is slick with perspiration from the lights as I slide my hands down to the tops of her leggings. Hooking my thumbs over her leggings, I slide them down her legs.

She leans her elbows back on the couch so her breasts are sticking out and her head is tilted back. She knows how to pose, and this position puts her body on full display.

"You're beautiful." I know I sound like a record on repeat, but there's no other word for her. "You look like a Ruben's painting."

She smiles. "You see me with an artist's eye."

I shake my head. "I see you as a man who wants you to be his."

I draw my gaze away from her body and look her in the eye. "I want all of you, Adalee. I have since the day I first saw you on the runway a year ago. This isn't just a one-time thing; I want you as my woman."

"I'd like that." She looks down quickly, and I freeze.

"There's something else, isn't there?" She nods. I catch her chin in my hand and gently lift her face so she's looking at me. "You can tell me, baby."

She swallows nervously. "I'm a virgin."

"Oh baby."

A shot of heat goes straight to my dick at the words. I ache with longing to claim her. To be the first to have her. The animal in me wants to rip her panties off and break down her virgin walls. But the man in me knows to be gentle with her.

I gather her in my arms and pull her toward me. "Don't worry, baby. We'll take it slow." I run my hand around her waist. "But I will have you today."

I crash my lips into hers, and this time it's harder, more urgent.

I push her back against the couch and work my mouth down her body, exploring her curves until I'm at the top of her panties. I slide them off her legs and her scent fills my nostrils, sweet and earthy and driving me crazy.

I kneel before her and part her legs with my hands. She opens up for me and I kiss her thighs, feeling the skin quiver under my touch. My dick aches for her, but I go slowly, working up to the sweet spot between her legs.

My hand slides up to her slick pussy and the small patch of hair. She's damp under my touch, and I kiss her gently as my fingers stroke her.

She's leaning back and moaning at my touch. The sweet sound is like a calling card for my dick, but I'll take my time, make her first time special.

Her swollen pussy parts under my tongue, and I dart into her glistening hole. The sweet tangy taste fills my mouth and makes my body ache with longing. My fingers rub against her slickness as I lick her delicate folds.

I glance up at her and she's leaning against the couch with her eyes closed, one hand rolling circles on her nipple.

The sight of her pleasuring herself makes me hot with desire. I turn my attention back to her sweet pussy and pick up the pace. I need to make her cum because I need to be inside her, and I don't know how much longer I can hold back.

I slide my finger into her hole and she closes around me, her pussy sucking me into its warmth. She cries out as I lick her clit while my finger moves in and out of her delicate folds.

She sits forward, her eyes dark with desire, and tangles her fingers in my hair, drawing me toward her with every finger thrust. I push a second finger into her tight slit, and she cries out as push deeper.

My tongue rubs against her clit as I fuck her with my fingers. Suddenly she grips the back of my head and gives a high-pitched cry. Her pussy gushes wetness onto my tongue as her orgasm runs through her.

I keep up the pressure for a few moments until she stops trembling. When I slide my fingers out, I hold them to my mouth and lick her sweet nectar.

The taste of her makes my dick pulse, and she watches me dreamily as I unbutton my jeans. I slide my pants off, and her eyes go wide when she sees my dick standing to attention.

"You ready for me, baby?"

Adalee nods.

I angle her body so she's laying before me on the rug. I feast my eyes on her soft curves, full breasts, and that sweet, sweet pussy.

"So beautiful," I whisper.

She parts her legs for me and I kneel over her, lining my cock up with her opening. I run my dick over her entrance, covering my tip in her wet pussy juice.

"Will it hurt?" she whimpers.

"Maybe a little, just for a moment. Then it will feel good."

I slide the tip in, and she's so tight I almost snap. "Just relax and let me in, baby."

She sits up on her elbows. "I want to watch you going into me."

The words give me a thrill, and I push forward a little more. I suck in my breath as her pussy closes around me.

"You feel so good."

I'm pressing against her virgin barrier. One more thrust and I'll be in. My heart races as I look at her. "Are you ready to be mine?"

Adalee's eyes are hooded with desire. "I'm ready, Hayden."

I drive into her, and she cries out as my dick plows through her virgin walls. The heat and tightness are too much, and I almost lose control. I slide all the way in and pause inside her, letting her pussy adjust.

She lies back and lifts her legs, curling them around me. I grab her thigh and hold it as I slide out and slam back into her, claiming her as mine.

I lift her legs up, letting me go deeper. Her eyes go

wide with every thrust, and her moans get higher and shorter.

No longer aware of anything else I fuck her hard, lost in the sensation of her. Filling her up and coating my dick in her virgin juices.

I'm pounding into her now, watching her breasts jiggle with every move. Her mouth forms an "O" shape as her high-pitched cries build with her pleasure, spurring me on.

She cries out as she comes, and her pussy convulses. It sends me over the edge and my cum shoots deep inside her, a sweet release into her hot, wet depths.

She lowers her legs, and I pull out slowly and lay next to her. She looks sleepy and dreamy and content.

"You're beautiful," I say again. "And you're mine now."

"Yes," she says simply and closes her eyes, falling asleep in my arms.

5

ADALEE

he next day I'm humming to myself as I push open the door to the cafe. A smile plays on my lips remembering how Hayden made my body feel, and there's a warm tug in my core just thinking about it.

I spot Sophie, scrolling through her phone at a table by the window, and I head over. We're meeting to discuss the photo shoot we're doing for Stella in a few weeks. Stella's in the businesswomen's network and we're helping get her fashion line for plus sized women up and running.

I usually enjoy a good chat with Sophie but I already know I'm keeping this to myself; it's too private, too intimate. I'm not ready to share, not even with Sophie.

She looks up as I sit down, and the smile drops off my face. "Hon, what's wrong?"

She flips her phone over quickly and bites her lip not saying anything.

"What is it?" I put my hand over hers anxious for my friend. "You can tell me anything."

She stares at me with her brow wrinkled but doesn't say anything.

"Is it your mom?"

She shakes her head and seems to snap out of it. "No, everything's fine with me." She takes a deep breath. "It's you."

I frown, not understanding what she means. "It's me? What do you mean?"

"Adalee, someone's got nude pictures of you," she blurts out. "They're circulating them online."

My stomach clenches, and my blood goes cold.

"Kris, one of the other photographers saw them and told me. I haven't seen them; I don't want to."

There's a thumping in my ears, and she sounds like she's talking from far away. "Kris saw them?" I ask dumbly. I know Kris, I've worked with him, he's one of the good guys but I still don't want him to see me nude. I don't want anyone to see me nude, apart from Hayden. Hayden, that lying asshole.

"He's trying to trace them, find out where they came from."

"I know where they came from." The coldness has turned to fury.

"Adalee, you didn't pose nude, did you?"

It's the golden rule of modeling. Don't let a photographer talk you into posing nude. My mother warned me, and I didn't listen. I let myself get sucked into Hayden's sweet talk and gave everything to him. I trusted him, and he betrayed me.

"Hayden," I whisper.

Sophie looks confused. "I thought Hayden was one of the good ones." She shakes her head. "Just goes to show you can't trust anyone."

I stand up, pushing my chair back so hard it falls to the floor. "I have to go."

Feeling numb, I walk out of the cafe. Sophie scrambles to pick up the chair calling after me, but I ignore her.

I go straight to my car, and it's not until I'm at home with the door shut behind me that I allow the tears to fall.

I'm still crying an hour later when my phone rings. It's him, Hayden. I almost let it go to voice mail, but I answer it at the last minute. I won't give him the satisfaction of being ignored.

"Hey, baby," he says.

My mind reels at his audacity. "Don't you dare say that to me."

He's silent, and I push on. "After what you did. I trusted you."

"What are you talking about?" he sounds generally confused which shows how good an actor her is.

"You know what I'm talking about. I thought you were different. I thought you were someone I could trust. But you're just the same as every other sleaze bag in this industry who thinks they can treat models however they like."

"Adalee, I don't..."

"Don't waste your breath."

I hang up. My heart's pounding, and you're supposed to feel better when you let out your anger, but I don't.

The phone rings again, and this time I turn it off. I sink to the floor with my hands in my head. What will Momma think of me?

6

HAYDEN

The call goes straight to voicemail, and I leave another message.

"Adalee, it's Hayden. I'm not sure why you're upset. Please give me a call. Talk to me."

I hang up and pace my room. I thought we shared something special yesterday. It was special for me. So special I think I may be in love with Adalee. And I'm sure she felt that special connection too.

Something must have happened.

If she won't talk to me, I need to find someone who will. I go through my phone and find Sophie's number. I've worked with her a few times, and I've seen them together.

She picks up on the first ring.

"Sophie. It's Hayden here, the photographer."

"I know who you are, you asshole. How dare you do that to a sweet girl like Adalee? You're a fucking..."

I hold the phone away from my ear as her tirade continues. It's a full minute at least before I hear her voice falter.

"Sophie, I'm not sure what you think I've done. I think there's been a misunderstanding..."

"A misunderstanding!?..."

She goes into another rant, and I hold the phone away again until I hear her stop.

"Please, just tell me what I'm supposed to have done."

"Nude photos! You ass hat!"

It takes a while to coax it out of her, but finally I get the whole story. Someone's shared nudes of Adalee, and she thinks it's me.

As if I'd do that to her. The picture of her exposing her breast has already been wiped off my camera, the only copy encrypted in a password protected folder on my MacBook. The only person who's ever seeing that photo is me.

My vein in my neck is pulsing when I hang up with Sophie.

Adalee swore she'd never done nude photography before, and she told me she was a virgin. Maybe it was all a line, and she is just like the other girls.

I shake my head to clear it. No, not my Adalee. Something is not right here.

Next, I call Kris, the photographer Sophie said saw the nudes. He reluctantly agrees to send me the picture he saw. I pace my apartment as I wait, dreading what

I'm about to see. My phone buzzes, and I watch the image download, my heart in my throat.

It's Adalee all right, her wide eyes, full lips, that penetrating gaze straight down the lens. But that's not her body. The breasts are too small. The curves aren't there.

I peer closely at the screen. It's a Photoshop job. Someone's taken her head and put it on another model's body. They've done a decent enough job; you can't see where they've joined it. But the lighting's slightly different on the face than on the body, and the angle of her head doesn't quite match the pose. All details that the average horny guy wouldn't notice.

The twitch in my neck starts, and I squeeze my phone so hard the screen cracks.

I'm going to find out who did this, and he's going to pay.

7
ADALEE

It's later that night, and I'm curled up on the couch with my spoon in a tub of ice cream watching re-runs of *Friends*. The doorbell rings, and I frown as I set the half-melted tub on the coffee table.

I hitch up my sweatpants and run a hand through my hair. I've got no idea who could be visiting at this time.

I pull the door open, and Hayden's standing there. Anger flares in my chest at the same time as my body tingles at the sight of him.

He steps into the light, and I gasp. There's blood dripping from his nose, and his hand is bloody and bruised. "What happened?"

"Can I come in?"

I open the door reluctantly, and he follows me into the kitchen. I grab a paper towel and he takes it gratefully, pressing it against his nose.

As he tries to stop the blood, I examine him more carefully. The knuckles on one hand are scrapped raw with dark bruises under the skin. His nose looks broken, and there's a cut under his left eye.

"Have you been in a fight?"

He nods warily. "Something like that."

I fold my arms across my chest. "Well, I don't know why you came here." A thought occurs to me. "Or even how you knew where I lived."

"Sophie."

"Sophie gave you my address?" I am going to kill that girl. Why the hell would she give my address to Hayden.

"Relax." He holds up one hand. "It was under duress."

My eyes go wide. "You beat up Sophie?" This guy's more of an asshole then I realized.

"What? No." He snort laughs, then winces as blood spurts out of his nose. "Of course I didn't beat up Sophie. But when she heard who I did beat up, she was happy to give me your address."

My eyes narrow in suspicion and I grab a saucepan from the drying rack and hold it up like a weapon. I have no idea what he's capable of. "What have you done?"

He holds a hand up. "I know why you were mad at me."

"I trusted you." The hurt wells up inside me, and I blink back tears.

"It wasn't me, Adalee, I would never share our pictures."

I want to believe him but how could it be anyone else? "No one else had access to those pictures."

"I've seen the pictures. It was a bad Photoshop job. Your head on someone else's body."

I stare at him as the words sink in. "You mean you didn't circulate those pictures?"

"Of course I didn't."

The tight ball that's been sitting in my stomach all day starts to loosen. "Someone put my head on someone else's body. Why would they do that?"

He shrugs. "Because some guys are assholes."

I slump against the bench. It's a relief that it wasn't Hayden, but it doesn't change the fact that there are pictures out there that look like me in the nude.

"I found out who did it," he says quietly. "It was another photographer. He was trying to show off that he had gotten the Viking Ice Queen nude."

I shudder at the nickname, made up by men whose egos I've hurt by not sleeping with them.

"I paid him a visit," continues Hayden. "Convinced him to delete the files."

"How did you do that?" But I already know the answer.

He puts his hand on my arm. "No one disrespects you like that, Adalee. Or any woman. The guy needed to be taught a lesson."

His expression is hard, but his touch is gentle. He stood up for me, he protected me, and he's got a bloody nose to show for it.

"Let me clean you up."

I drag a chair into the kitchen "Sit down, but don't get any blood on the fabric," I instruct.

I grab a flannel from the cupboard and run a bowl of warm water.

"Looks like he got you a few good hits." I dab at the cut on his face. "And your nose is probably broken."

"Yeah, he wasn't too happy to see me. He didn't get what I was so upset about. Got me a few good hits before I overpowered him, dragged him to his computer, and made him delete the files."

"But it's not just the files." I sigh. "Those pictures were posted all over the web. They could be anywhere."

Hayden shakes his head, then winces. "I watched as he deleted them online. He only posted to one group of guys. His photographer buddies."

"Are you sure?"

"He's got his reputation to think of too. If that image got around, it wouldn't look good for him. He only wanted to brag to his industry friends."

I wring out the flannel and dab at his nose again. "I'm sorry you had to do that," I say quietly. "Thank you."

He reaches up and grabs my wrist. "I'd do anything for you, Adalee. I meant what I said yesterday."

He releases my wrist, and I look away. This morning I was floating on air I was so happy, but it's been an emotional day. I didn't think I could trust him, and I'm still feeling raw.

"What is it?" he asks, sensing my hesitation.

I drop the flannel in the bowl and come around to face him. "Yesterday was amazing, but it's all a bit overwhelming."

He winces, and this time it's not from the physical pain. I make myself keep talking before I change my mind.

"It all happened way too fast, Hayden. I like you, I really do, but I don't think I can be in a relationship right now."

Tears threaten to sting my eyes, and I blink them back. "I don't even know if I want to be in this industry anymore after what's happened today."

"Baby, I can understand that." His understanding makes my heart soften. But I need to do this, I need to prove to myself I can be strong.

"I just need some time on my own."

Hayden stands up and takes my hand in his. "I know you're the woman for me, Adalee. And I'll do whatever it takes to make you see that. If you need some time, you take it. I'll be right here waiting, and whenever you're ready I'm here for you."

He gives me a kiss on the cheek, and part of me wants to hold onto him and never let him go, but the other part of me knows I need to figure this out on my own.

"Goodbye Adalee," he says as he goes out the door. It shuts behind him and I'm left alone, wondering if I've just let the best thing in my life go.

Warily, I slink back to the couch where ice cream and *Friends* are waiting.

8

HAYDEN

It's four weeks later, and I'm smiling at guests as they come through the gallery door. It's opening night for my first exhibition showcasing my portraits.

"She has a certain quality. The lens loves her," says Maria, a friend of mine who's a film producer. She's sipping a glass of champagne while staring contemplatively at one of Adalee's photos. "You said she'd be here tonight?"

"I hope so." I've given Adalee her space over the last few weeks, but I've let her know I'm thinking about her. I've sent roses and a few messages, but I've mostly given her the space she needs.

I'm happy to wait. I've known since the moment I first saw her on the runway almost a year ago that we're meant to be together. If she needs a bit longer to figure it out, that's fine by me.

I invited her to the opening tonight, and my stomach's in knots wondering if she'll come. She's the star of the show with her portraits taking up the main exhibition space. Besides, I want her to meet Maria.

I'm talking to the gallery owner when I see Adalee come through the door. She's taller than most guests, and even though she's dressed casually in a simple skirt and sweater, she lights up the room.

My heartbeat quickens, and there's a tug in my cock.

Heads turn and there's an excited murmur; she really is the star tonight.

"I'm glad you could make it." I kiss her cheek and hand her a glass of champagne. The smell of her perfume makes me dizzy, and it's all I can do not to take her in my arms.

She looks around wide-eyed, taking in the photos of herself.

"Hayden, they're amazing. You really have a talent."

She walks up to one of the photos. In it she's leaning on the couch, her mouth slightly open, laugh lines crinkling her eyes.

"That one's my favorite. I caught you laughing."

"It's so natural looking," she says in wonder. "Those lines around my eyes would usually be photoshopped out."

"A shame, isn't it? I like seeing the natural you."

She smiles. "They're really good."

I take her hand because I can't resist touching her. "I'm glad you're here."

"I wouldn't miss it," she says, squeezing my hand.

Maria catches my eye, and I beckon her over. "Adalee, I want you to meet a friend of mine. Maria is a film producer; I've been telling her all about you."

"It's nice to meet you in the flesh," says Maria, eyeing Adalee appraisingly. "Hayden's been telling me about you the amazing actress I must meet."

Adalee gives me a thankful look. I leave them talking as I mingle with other guests.

As I work my way around the room, my gaze always comes back to Adalee. She's talking excitedly with Maria, and when they move apart, I go to her again.

"I've got an audition." The smile spreads across her whole face. "Maria asked me to audition for the new series she's working on."

"That's great news!"

"And I wouldn't just be the big girl eating cake. It's a real part. She's going to send me the script tomorrow."

"I'm happy for you."

"And I have you to thank."

I shrug my shoulders. "Maria loved your look in these photos. She couldn't wait to meet you."

"Thank you." She kisses me on the cheek, and I get a whiff of perfume again.

This time I can't resist. I slide my arm around her

waist and pull her toward me. "Have dinner with me tonight."

"Actually, I was thinking..." She hesitates, and my heart sinks. "I was thinking maybe you could come back to my place after this."

My eyes shoot up. "Really?"

"I'm ready," she says simply.

"Then let's go."

"You can't leave your exhibition." She looks appalled.

"My agent will take care of any sales. Let's go."

I take her hand in mine and lead her toward the door. No one seems to notice as we slip out into the night.

9

ADALEE

My hand's trembling as I let Hayden in the door to my apartment. Over the past four weeks, all I've thought about is his hands on my body, his mouth on my most intimate parts, and his dick sliding into me.

It's been hard not to go to him sooner, but I wanted to wait, to be sure.

Now, as he follows me into the kitchen, I'm aware of him behind me. His heavy tread, the sound of his breathing.

"Do you want a drink" I turn and lean on the countertop.

"No." He shakes his head and takes a step toward me. "I want you."

He puts his hands on either side of me, trapping me between his strong arms.

My heartbeat goes up a notch as I look into his eyes, full of love and want. His lips crash into mine, insistent and passionate, and I kiss him back, pulling at his lips.

His arms go around me and he pulls me to him, pressing his body against mine.

"Adalee," he whispers into my ear. "You're mine."

The words send a thrill through me, and I tilt my head back as his mouth slides down my neck, nibbling on my soft skin and sending tingles shooting all the way down to the place between my legs.

I run my hands up his neck and into his shaggy hair. His hardness presses against me, sending a gush of wetness to my panties.

His hands slide under my sweater, and he pulls it over my head. I'm wearing a red lace bra, and I lean back on the counter as his gaze sweeps over my breasts.

"You're beautiful."

"You should see the matching set." I give him a cheeky smile, and he raises an eyebrow.

"Don't mind if I do." He reaches behind me and slowly unzips my skirt. I let it drop to the floor and step out of it. Now I'm wearing nothing but the lacy underwear set and my high heels.

He sucks in his breath while his eyes travel over my body. I feel sexy and confident and powerful.

"Oh baby, you are stunning."

"Follow me." I hold out a hand and lead him into the

living room. We stop in front of the sofa, and I pull off his t-shirt, running my hands over his firm chest and tangling them in the tiny curls of hair.

I unbuckle his jeans and slide them to the floor. His dick sticks out of his underwear, and I slowly slide them off too.

"Sit down." I push his chest, and he sits on the middle part of the sofa.

I stand over him, swaying my hips from side to side, loving the way his eyes are moving over my body. His lustful gaze is making me wet between the legs.

Looking him directly in the eye, I hook my thumbs over the top of my panties and slide them slowly down my legs. I step out of them and straighten up. Now I'm just in my bra and high heels.

He reaches out a hand, and his voice is husky when he speaks. "Come here, baby."

I straddle him on the couch, and he pulls me toward him. His dick shoots up between us, and I press myself to him so I feel his shaft against my pussy lips.

He moans at the contact and pulls me in for a kiss.

As our lips collide his hands move over my body, moving up my back and into my hair. Wherever he touches me I'm on fire, my skin tingling and my pussy gushing with wetness.

His hands go around my ass, and he lifts me up.

"You ready for me, baby?"

In answer, I grab the base of his dick and line him

up with my needy pussy. He lowers me slightly so his tip grazes the inside of my pussy. I suck him in hungrily, wanting more.

"Let me ride you." My voice comes out pleading.

"If that's what you want, baby."

He lets go of my ass, and I slide slowly down his cock, my hungry pussy taking all of him in.

My pussy's on fire as he fills me up and I lean into him, our bodies pressed together. We rock for a moment, joined together. Then I lift myself up, slowly easing him in and out.

His hand slides up to my breast, and he pulls the lace aside. I lean forward, and he takes the nipple in his mouth.

I gasp at the sensation; he's flicking my nipple with his tongue as his dick slides in and out of me. His other hand grabs my ass and he pulls me down onto him, taking back some control.

I moan as he lifts me up and down on his cock. My clit presses against him with every thrust, and I can feel my climax building.

His pace is relentless, in and out, slamming into me as he flicks my nipple. His groans get deeper, and it sets me over the edge.

I cry out as I come, and he joins me. I feel his seed shoot into me as our bodies join in pleasure. There's nothing else in the world but the two of us in this moment.

I collapse against him and we stay that way for a while, happy and content. When we do finally move it's to creep into my bed, where we make love again and fall asleep holding each other. When we wake the next morning, it's to a new world, a world where we're together. The first day of the rest of our lives.

EPILOGUE

ADALEE

Five years later...

I push open the door to the gallery and let Isla run ahead of me.

"Daddy, daddy!" she calls excitedly.

Hayden turns from where he's directing the hanging of one of his pictures and scoops her up in his arms.

"Hey, sweetie." He kisses her nose and she giggles, her curly dark hair flopping around her face.

"How are my best girls today?" He sets her down on the floor and gives me a kiss on the cheek. His hand slips around my pregnant belly, and his mouth moves to mine.

We share a tender kiss until Isla pushes between us.

"We brought you lunch, Daddy."

We laugh as we pull apart, my jealous daughter making sure I don't get more attention than she does.

"What did you bring me?" He takes the brown lunch bag from me and crouches down so he's at Isla's height.

"Let's see. Is it sandwiches?"

He peers into the bag, and Isla jumps up and down excitedly. "It is sandwiches! Peanut butter and jelly."

"My favorite."

While they get the sandwiches out, I take a look around the gallery.

I love it when I'm between shoots and can come and meet Hayden for lunch.

I got the part when I auditioned for Maria. It was a small speaking role but I've worked my way up, and in her latest series they wrote a part especially for me.

I love having a role where I'm not judged for my size. I'm just a character in a story, and it's got nothing to do with being plus sized.

The only plus sized modeling I do these days are for Stella's clothing range. Her clothing business is growing since she met her hot angel investor and me and Sophie still do all her shoots.

Hayden also left the world of fashion photography behind. He does photography portraits now, mostly as commissions from celebrity clients. But his favorite subject is still me.

The opening of his latest exhibition is tonight, and every thing's just about set up. We have friends arriving from Maple Springs for the show. Some of the girls from the women's business network are coming and also Heather, a model from Maple Falls, the small mountain town not far from Maple Springs. Hayden and I helped launch Heather's career a few years ago. Her husband is also a photographer and a friend of Hayden's. From what Heather's confided to me; our nude shoots are nothing compared to what they get up to!

It will be nice to have friends in town but for the next few hours, I want to enjoy my husband and the quiet gallery space before it gets busy.

I take a wander, browsing the photos.

As usual, there are a lot of me, this time with my pregnant belly on display.

I stop in front of one that's taken from a side angle. I'm leaning back, looking straight ahead. My body is naked, but my arms cover my breasts and my legs cross over so nothing is seen.

The focus is on the round curve of my stomach and the life that's growing inside. It was taken just two weeks ago, and this is the first time I've seen it blown up to life size.

I don't hear Hayden come up behind me until his arms slide around my waist. "This is my favorite."

"I like it too."

"You look so powerful, like a goddess."

I laugh. "I like it because it's a symbol of mother-hood, my greatest achievement."

"Whatever you want to see in it, there's no denying you look beautiful."

His hand slips up my stomach and cups my breast.

I glance around quickly, but Isla's sharing her sandwich with the gallery owner.

"Are you taking her home for a nap soon?" His thumb brushes over my nipple.

"Right after lunch."

"I might come back with you." His lips brush the nape of my neck.

"I think you should."

"Daddy, you didn't eat your sandwich!" We break away as Isla comes running over with a sandwich in her hand.

He takes it off her solemnly. "Thank you, sweetheart."

As she leads him back to the lunch bag, he turns to me. His look is full of love and promise and want. "Nap time," he mouths, raising his eyebrows.

I nod, and he turns back to our daughter. I watch them together, my heart full of love and my body tingling with anticipation.

GET YOUR FREE BOOK

Sign up to the Sadie King mailing list for a FREE book!

You'll be the first to hear about exclusive offers, bonus content and all the news from Sadie King.

Allie is a bonus book in the Curvy Girl Can series exclusive to my newsletter subscribers.

To claim your free book visit:

authorsadieking.com/bonus-scenes

Sadie King is a USA Today Best Selling Author of short instalove romance.

She lives in New Zealand with her ex-military husband and raucous young son.

When she's not writing she loves catching waves with her son, running along the beach, and drinking good wine, preferably with a book in hand.